Dear Parents:

Congratulations! Your child is taking the first steps on an exciting journey. The destination? Independent reading!

STEP INTO READING® will help your child get there. The program offers five steps to reading success. Each step includes fun stories and colorful art or photographs. In addition to original fiction and books with favorite characters, there are Step into Reading Non-Fiction Readers, Phonics Readers and Boxed Sets, Sticker Readers, and Comic Readers—a complete literacy program with something to interest every child.

Learning to Read, Step by Step!

Ready to Read   Preschool–Kindergarten
• big type and easy words • rhyme and rhythm • picture clues
For children who know the alphabet and are eager to begin reading.

Reading with Help   Preschool–Grade 1
• basic vocabulary • short sentences • simple stories
For children who recognize familiar words and sound out new words with help.

Reading on Your Own   Grades 1–3
• engaging characters • easy-to-follow plots • popular topics
For children who are ready to read on their own.

Reading Paragraphs   Grades 2–3
• challenging vocabulary • short paragraphs • exciting stories
For newly independent readers who read simple sentences with confidence.

Ready for Chapters   Grades 2–4
• chapters • longer paragraphs • full-color art
For children who want to take the plunge into chapter books but still like colorful pictures.

STEP INTO READING® is designed to give every child a successful reading experience. The grade levels are only guides; children will progress through the steps at their own speed, developing confidence in their reading. The F&P Text Level on the back cover serves as another tool to help you choose the right book for your child.

Remember, a lifetime love of reading starts with a single step!

Text copyright © 2019 by Amy Krouse Rosenthal Revocable Trust
Cover art and interior illustrations copyright © 2019 by Brigette Barrager
Written by Candice Ransom
Illustrations by Lissy Marlin

Visit us on the Web!
StepIntoReading.com
rhcbooks.com

Educators and librarians, for a variety of teaching tools, visit us at RHTeachersLibrarians.com

Library of Congress Cataloging-in-Publication Data is available upon request.
ISBN 978-1-9848-5023-2 (trade) — ISBN 978-1-9848-5024-9 (lib. bdg.) —
ISBN 978-1-9848-5025-6 (ebook)

Printed in the United States of America
10 9 8 7 6 5 4 3 2 1

This book has been officially leveled by using the F&P Text Level Gradient™ Leveling System.

Uni the UNICORN
Uni's First Sleepover

an Amy Krouse Rosenthal book
pictures based on art by Brigette Barrager

Random House 🏠 New York

Tonight is Uni's
first sleepover.
Uni cannot wait!

Uni trots
to the top
of Sunny Hill.
Goldie, Pinkie, and
Silky are already there.

"Let's play
sparkle ball,"
says Goldie.
"I played it at
my last sleepover."

Goldie kicks
the ball to Uni.

Uni kicks it
into the mud.
Uni is out of
the game.

Uni does not mind.
The sleepover
is still fun.

"I can make colors
when I run,"
Pinkie says.
"I learned how at
my last sleepover."

"I want to do that,"

says Uni.

Pinkie runs fast.
She makes a
pink streak.

Uni runs fast, too.
Uni does not make
a pink streak.

Uni does not mind.
The sleepover
is still fun.

They go to
Deep Pond.
"I can kick a rock
across the pond,"
Silky says.

"I did it at
my last sleepover."
Silky's rock flies
like a bird
over Deep Pond.

It is Uni's turn.
Uni's rock lands
in the water.

Uni is not having

fun now.

The sun sets.

It is dark.

The unicorns
lie down on
their blankets.
Stars glow above.

Then clouds
cover the sky.
The stars are gone.

An owl hoots.

It is *very* dark.

Uni hears
someone crying.
"What is wrong?"
Uni asks.

"The dark scares me,"
says Goldie.

"It scares us, too,"
say Pinkie and Silky.

23

"I know!" says Uni.
"We can make a tent
with our blankets
to feel safe."

The blanket tent helps.
But the unicorns
are still awake.

So Uni tells
a story.
It is about
the sparkling sun
and a rainbow

and birds flying
across the sky.
One by one,
the unicorns
close their eyes.

Bright sun
wakes them.
It is a new day.

"You tell great
stories, Uni!"
says Goldie.
"I cannot wait
to hear more!"

Uni is happy.

Uni is good

at something, too!

Uni is excited for
the next sleepover.
"Let's play
sparkle ball!"
Uni says.